4 u

Postman Pat
Takes a Message

Story by **John Cunliffe** Pictures by **Celia Berridge**

from the original Television designs by **Ivor Wood**

 ANDRE DEUTSCH

First published 1983 by
André Deutsch Limited
105 Great Russell Street London WC1
Second impression March 1984
Third impression April 1984

Phototypeset by Tradespools Limited, Frome, Somerset
Printed in Great Britain by Cambus Litho, East Kilbride, Scotland

ISBN 0-233-97547 0

The wind had been blowing and banging all night in Greendale. When morning came, Postman Pat set out on his round. He drove his red van and his cat, Jess, sat by his side. What a mess the wind had made!

All along the valley, branches had been blown off the trees. Many were scattered on the roads and Pat had to dodge the big ones as he drove along. By Greendale Farm, a whole tree had blown down, just missing Peter Fogg's cottage. Some telephone-wires were broken too.

"Dear me," said Pat, "that's a nuisance. There'll be a fair number of telephones out of action, now."

Then, as they came to the vicarage, he stopped.

"I wonder if the Reverend kept that stamp for me? Better pop in and see him . . . I hope he remembered."

The Reverend Timms was busy. He seemed to be packing his cases to go on holiday.

"Hello, Reverend!" called Pat. "I just popped in to see if you kept that Australian stamp for me, yesterday."

"Of course, Pat," said the Reverend Timms, "just the thing for your collection ..."

"Thanks," said Pat, "but where are you off to?"

"I'm off to London! To meet my sister, Elsie ... that's what the letter was all about ... she's flying over from Australia ... haven't seen her for years ... what a rush! Now, *where* did I put that stamp? Ah, *here* it is."

"Thank you," said Pat.

The Reverend picked the telephone up to see if it was working. No luck! "Such a nuisance," he said. "The phone's not working, so I'll have to rush round and see everyone, to cancel the church meetings while I'm away. Such a bother, with a train to catch . . ."

"It's this wind," said Pat. "It's brought the wires down."

"Well, I'll just have to hurry. The train goes at ten o'clock."

"I hope you get round in time," said Pat. "Cheerio! Have a good trip! Thanks for the stamp!"

Pat was on his way.

He called at the post-office for the letters.
"Morning, Mrs. Goggins! I'm not late, am I?"

"Not really," said Mrs. Goggins, "but I thought you might have trouble getting through, what with all these trees being blown down."

Pat told Mrs. Goggins about the Reverend Timms' letter, and his trip to London, and his telephone being out of order.

"Ee it's a bad job, isn't it," she said. Then her telephone began to ring.

"*My* phone's working, anyway. Hello – Greendale post-office here – who is it? Elsie Timms? Urgent message for the Reverend Timms? Yes . . . his phone *is* out of order . . . yes . . . your flight diverted to Manchester?"

"Oh dear," said Pat.

"You'll come on to Greendale by car? Yes . . . I'll ask our postman to dash over and tell the Reverend not to go to London after all – he might just catch him."

"I've got the message," said Pat. "Tell her I'm on my way."
"Bye, Pat! I hope you're on time. Bye!"
Pat dashed out to his van.
"Hold tight, Jess; it's full speed ahead."

Along the twisting roads they went, back to the vicarage. Pat knocked on the door, but the vicar had gone.

"I'll leave a note for him," said Pat, "in case he calls back before he catches his train. Let's see, he's sure to call on Miss Hubbard. We'll try and catch up with him there. Come on, Jess, we can take a short cut along the back road."

Pat jolted off along the bumpy back road to Miss Hubbard's. It was a very rough ride. And then, when they were almost there, the road was blocked by Peter Fogg's trailer. There wasn't even enough room to turn round and go back. So Pat jumped out, put Jess in his bag, and ran across the field to Miss Hubbard's cottage.

"Hello, Pat," said Miss Hubbard, "what's all the hurry, and where is your van?"

"Morning, Miss Hubbard," Pat panted, "I'm trying to catch up with the Reverend Timms. Have you seen him?"

"Oh, he went a few minutes ago. He's in a hurry too; he wants to catch a train."

"I must catch him before he does," said Pat. "I have an urgent message for him."

"He did say he was calling on Ted Glen. You might catch him there. Quick!
You can borrow my bike. Go on!"

Pat put Jess in the basket, and wobbled away, gathering speed. He called
over his shoulder –

"Thanks, Miss Hubbard! I'll try anything . . . hold tight, Jess!"

Pat whizzed, and jolted, and wobbled his way to Ted Glen's; but he couldn't stop when he arrived, and he crashed into the workshop-door, and tumbled in a heap on the floor.

"Hello, Pat, whatever are you doing?" said Ted. "Are you all right?"

"Yes, I think so. I'm trying to catch up with the Reverend."

"You're too late," said Ted. "The Reverend's gone; but he said he would call on Granny Dryden, before he catches his train." But when Pat tried the bike, the front wheel wouldn't go round.

"Leave it to me," said Ted. "I'll fettle it. You can borrow these roller-skates. I've just mended them. You'll fairly move when you get these on."

"Well, I said I'd try anything," said Pat, "and we must catch the Reverend before he catches his train. Thanks, Ted. Here we go again ... Ooooooooooops!"

Pat shot out of Ted's workshop like a rocket, and away along the road to Granny Dryden's. *But,* he had forgotten to ask Ted where the brakes were! When he came to a sharp bend in the road, he was going too fast to get round the bend, and too fast to stop. So he did a somersault over the gate and landed in a soft patch of mud.

Sam Waldron's van was coming along the road. The Reverend Timms was riding in it, as Sam was giving him a lift to the station.

"I thought I saw Pat dive over that gate," said Sam. He stopped his van to get a better look.

Then, Pat scrambled to his feet and waved to them.

"It *is* Pat," said Sam.

"Hello, Sam! . . . and Reverend!" called Pat. "I've caught you at last. Thank goodness you've not gone to London."

Pat told the Reverend all about his sister's phone message, and how he must not go to London after all, as she was coming straight to Greendale.

"Lord bless us," he said, "what a good thing you caught me in time. I'd have gone traipsing off to London and missed Elsie, and she would have been here looking for me! After all that rush, too! Never mind, all's well in the end. Thank you so much, Pat. Let's go home, Sam, and we'll have a nice cup of tea. Can we give you lift, Pat?"

But Peter Fogg came along, with his tractor and trailer. When he heard the story, he said,

"It's my fault that Pat had to leave his van. I left my trailer in the road. I'll give you a lift back to your van, Pat."

"And I'd better get along to meet my sister," said the Reverend Timms. "God speed! And thanks to all!"

So Pat and Jess rode back on the trailer. Pat was glad to see his van again. As for Jess, he never wanted to see a bike or a roller-skate again. He curled up thankfully on his seat, as Pat drove on his way. As they passed the vicarage, the Reverend was just carrying a suitcase in, with an Australian label on it.

"She's arrived," he said. "I was back just in time, thanks to you, Pat. And I found your pen on my doorstep."

"Thanks," said Pat. "I hope your sister enjoys her visit. Cheerio!"

"Thanks, Pat. Bye! Bye, Jess!"

"Now we'll get the letters delivered," said Pat to Jess. "That bothersome wind – it's made a real mischief of itself, to-day."